ALL THE WAYS TO BE SMART

Davina Bell & Allison Colpoys

SCRIBBLE

To dearest Belle,
the inspiration for this book,
thank you.
Love, Aunty Al

To dear Harry and Oscar, Sammy, Noah and
Christopher, Scarlett and Rapha, Rose and Magnolia,
Georgie, James and Ben, Sophia, Thomas and William,
Max and Genevieve, Hugo, Fergus and Indi.
You are all so smart!
Love, Aunty Beans

And to dear Esther,
we can't wait to see
all the ways you are smart.
Love, Al & Davina

The author and illustrator would like to say a heartfelt thank you to
Jeremy Wortsman and Lorelei Vashti for having us to stay at Jacky Winter Gardens,
where many ideas for this book were dreamed up.

The illustrations in this book were made
with ink, charcoal and pencil and digitally assembled

Typeset in Gill Sans

Published by Scribble, an imprint of Scribe Publications
2018 (Australia) and 2019 (UK and US)
Reprinted 2018 (twice), 2019 (twice)

18–20 Edward Street, Brunswick, Victoria 3056, Australia
2 John Street, Clerkenwell, London, WC1N 2ES, United Kingdom
3754 Pleasant Ave, Suite 100, Minneapolis, Minnesota 55409 USA

Text © Davina Bell, 2018
Illustrations © Allison Colpoys, 2018

Printed and bound in China by Imago

9781925713435 (Australian hardback)
9781911617556 (UK hardback)
9781911617877 (UK paperback)
9781947534964 (US hardback)

Catalogue records for this title are available from the
National Library of Australia and the British Library

scribblekidsbooks.com

I can't wait to share with you
how smart you are the whole day through.

Smart at drawing witches' hats,
smart at gluing wings on bats.

Smart at rhyme and telling time,
climbing trees and making slime.

Smart is not just ticks and crosses,
smart is building boats from boxes.

Painting patterns, wheeling wagons,
being mermaids, riding dragons.

Smart at drawing things with claws,
facts about the dinosaurs.
Folding up airplanes for flying…

Smart is kindness when there's crying.

Growing, throwing, bubble blowing.

Smart is knowing where you're going.

Finding treasures, flower picking…

Ukulele!

Finger clicking!

Smart at sharing, caring, scaring,
smart at picking what you're wearing.

Smart at saying hi and bye

to people when they feel all shy.

Crazy
dances!

Horsey
prances!

Feeling scared
but taking chances.

Jumping off
so you can fly!

Smart at asking
How? What? Why?

Smart at building ships to Mars,
drawing very pointy stars.

Knowing all the planet names,
making spacesuits that shoot flames.

Smart at matching
shapes in pairs,
like hexagons and
big blue squares.

Counting all the
way past forty,
being sorry when
you're naughty.

Smart at bugs
and squeezy hugs,

and mixing potions
up in mugs.

Making up new games with teams...

and floating off on
daytime dreams.

Smart is reading, writing, spelling, but it's also storytelling.

Finding things on all the pages...

sitting still and quiet for ages.

Smart is not
just being best
at spelling bees,
a tricky test.

Or knowing all
the answers ever…

Other things
are just as clever.

Every hour of every day,
we're smart in our
own special way.

And nobody
will ever do...

the very same smart things as you.